Goldsworthy and Mort
in
Summer Fun

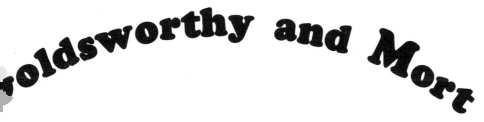

Goldsworthy and Mort

in

Summer Fun

by Marcia Vaughan

pictures by Linda Hendry

A Ready ☆ Set ☆ Read Book™

HarperCollins

Produced by Caterpillar Press

Ready ☆ Set ☆ Read is a trademark of
HarperCollins Publishers Ltd.

Text copyright © 1990 by Marcia Vaughan.
Illustrations copyright © 1990 by Linda Hendry.
All rights reserved.

Canadian Cataloguing in Publication Data

Vaughan, Marcia K.
     Goldsworthy & Mort — summer fun
1st ed.
"A ready set read book".
ISBN 0-00-617942-8

I. Hendry, Linda. II. Title.

PZ7.V383Go 1990   j823   C90-093555-3

For Brian Benedetti
M.V.

For Hez
L.H.

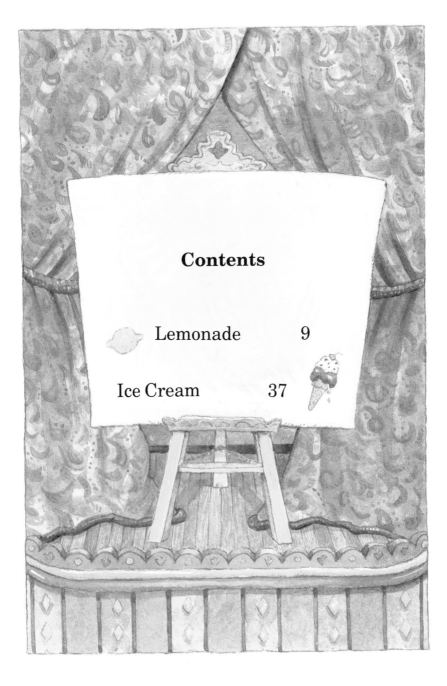

Contents

Lemonade   9

Ice Cream   37

LEMONADE

It was a warm summer day.

Goldsworthy and Mort

had a lemonade stand.

They were selling lemonade

for five cents a glass.

Goldsworthy put six glasses

and two money jars

on the counter.

"What happens now?"

Mort asked.

"Lots of thirsty animals

will come by,"

Goldsworthy explained.

"They will all want to buy

a glass of cool lemonade.

Soon the lemonade will be gone,

our jars will be full of money

and we will be rich."

"How rich?"

asked Mort.

Goldsworthy grinned.

"*Very* rich," he said.

"Good," said Mort.

"I am going to buy a boat.

A blue boat with

a mast and sails."

"And I am going to buy a racing car,"

Goldsworthy said.

"A yellow racing car with

a loud horn and shiny wheels."

Mort looked up the road.

He looked down the road.

He did not see any thirsty animals.

"I wonder who will buy

the first glass of lemonade,"

Mort said.

"I have five cents,"

said Goldsworthy. "I will."

Goldsworthy dropped his nickel

into Mort's jar.

Mort poured him

a glass of lemonade.

"Yum," said Goldsworthy.

"This is good.

You should try some, Mort."

Mort looked at the shiny coin

in the bottom of his jar.

"I will," he said.

Mort took the nickel out of his jar.

He tossed it into Goldsworthy's jar.

"We have sold two glasses,"

smiled Goldsworthy.

"We are getting richer."

Goldsworthy and Mort

sat for a long time.

It was hot.

It was quiet.

No one came by.

"This lemonade selling

is hard work,"

sighed Goldsworthy.

"Yes, it is,"

agreed Mort.

He wiped his brow.

"All this sitting.

All this waiting.

It makes me thirsty, Goldsworthy."

"Let me buy you a drink, Mort."

Goldsworthy took the nickel

out of his jar.

He dropped it into Mort's jar

and he poured his friend a drink.

"Delicious," said Mort.

"May I return the favor?"

"By all means,"

Goldsworthy agreed.

Mort handed the nickel

back to Goldsworthy.

He poured his friend a drink.

Goldsworthy looked

up and down the road.

"Maybe no one knows

we are selling lemonade today,"

he sighed.

"Then I will tell them,"

Mort said.

Mort ran up the road.

He ran down the road.

He ran up and down

and down and up,

over and over again.

"Did you find any thirsty animals?"
Goldsworthy asked.

"Yes," Mort huffed.

"I did," he puffed.

"Who?" Goldsworthy asked.

"Me!" panted Mort.

"May I borrow five cents?"

Goldsworthy took the nickel

out of his jar

and handed it to Mort.

"One lemonade, please,"

said Mort.

"And make it a big one."

Mort dropped the nickel

into Goldsworthy's jar.

Goldsworthy poured

a glass of lemonade

for his thirsty friend.

"Now we have only

one glass of lemonade

left to sell,"

smiled Goldsworthy.

Suddenly Mort looked worried.

"What if two animals come

at the same time?"

Mort asked.

"What if they both want

a glass of lemonade?"

"They might argue,"

said Goldsworthy.

"They might fight,"

said Mort.

"Quick, Goldsworthy!"

said Mort.

"Drink the last glass of lemonade

before we have trouble."

Goldsworthy did just that.

"The lemonade is gone,"

he said.

"We must be rich.

Let's count our money."

Goldsworthy and Mort

turned their jars

upside down.

One shiny nickel

rattled across the counter.

"Great galloping gumballs!"

gasped Goldsworthy.

"We've only made five cents

all day long!"

"You cannot buy a boat

with five cents,"

said Mort.

"You cannot buy a racing car either,"

sighed Goldsworthy.

"There is only one thing

you can buy for five cents,"

said Mort.

"You are right,"

Goldsworthy cried with delight.

"Let's get one right now."

Goldsworthy and Mort

took their nickel

and ran all the way

to the store.

"One bottle of lemonade, please!"

they laughed.

ICE CREAM

It was a hot day at the beach.

Goldsworthy and Mort

sat in their chairs

watching the waves roll in.

"I'd like something

creamy and cold

and sweet to eat,"

Goldsworthy sighed.

"An ice cream cone

is what I'd like.

My favorite flavor is—"

"Wait!" shouted Mort.

He jumped out of his chair.

"Don't tell me.

I can guess

what your favorite flavor is."

"You can?"

asked Goldsworthy.

"Yes,"

boasted Mort.

"I am a very good guesser."

Mort hurried across the hot sand

to the snack cart.

Then he hurried back again.

"Here is a chocolate ice cream cone.

Your favorite kind,"

Mort said proudly.

Goldsworthy did not smile back.

"But Mort," he said,

"chocolate is *not*

my favorite flavor."

Mort's whiskers drooped.

"I do not like chocolate

very much myself,"

he said.

"Don't look so sad,"

said Goldsworthy.

"Chocolate is not

my favorite flavor,

but I will eat it anyway."

"Do that," grinned Mort,

"while I get you

a different kind."

"Mort, my favorite kind is—"

Mort threw his paws

over his ears.

"Don't tell me, Goldsworthy.

I can guess,"

said Mort.

Minutes later Mort returned

looking very pleased

with himself.

A cone with five scoops

of ice cream

wobbled in his fist.

The first scoop was raspberry.

The second scoop was blueberry.

The third scoop was orange swirl.

The fourth scoop was pineapple.

And the fifth scoop was

raisin rocky-road ripple.

"Ho, ho," laughed Mort.

"This cone has to have

your favorite flavor."

But Goldsworthy did not laugh.

"No, Mort,"

he said.

"That cone does *not* have

my favorite flavor on it."

Mort gasped.

"Not one of these is

your favorite flavor?"

Mort asked.

"No,"

said Goldsworthy.

"Are you sure?"

Mort asked.

"*Very* sure,"

said Goldsworthy.

Mort stared at the

ice cream cone.

He watched the ice cream

dripping on to the sand.

"I don't like any of

these flavors either,"

he said.

Mort looked like he was

going to cry.

"Don't worry a whisker, Mort,"

said Goldsworthy.

"I will eat this ice cream cone too."

All afternoon

Mort tried to guess

Goldsworthy's favorite flavor

of ice cream.

"Maple nut?"

"Candy corn crunch?"

"Citrus surprise?"

"Bubblegum jumble?"

And all afternoon

Goldsworthy gulped and gobbled

Mort's mistakes.

The sun was slowly sinking

as Mort bought

the last flavor of ice cream

from the snack cart.

Mort was so excited that

he did not watch

where he was going.

Thunk!

He tripped on a stick.

Whizz!

Up flew the ice cream.

Plop!

It came down

right on top of

an ant hill.

"Jumping jellybeans!"

cried Mort.

"Goldsworthy's ice cream

is covered with

hundreds of little black ants."

Mort felt awful.

He trudged up to Goldsworthy.

He held out the cone with

the bumpy black blob on it.

"Is this ice cream?"

Goldsworthy asked.

Mort nodded.

"Is this plain old

everyday vanilla ice cream?"

Goldsworthy asked.

Mort nodded again.

"Is this plain old

everyday vanilla ice cream

covered with hundreds of

tiny black ants?"

"Yes,"

Mort sighed sadly. "It is."

Goldsworthy jumped

up and down.

He danced around Mort.

"You *are* a good guesser, Mort,"

he sang.

"Because my favorite kind
of ice cream is plain old
everyday vanilla
covered with ants!"
"Hurray!" cheered Mort.
He pushed the cone into
Goldsworthy's paws.

Suddenly Goldsworthy's face

turned as green as seaweed.

"I am very sorry, Mort,"

said Goldsworthy.

"But my stomach doesn't feel

like any more ice cream today.

You can eat it."

Mort stared at the

wiggly black ants.

Mort thought about

all the ice cream

that Goldsworthy

had eaten for him.

He closed his eyes.

He held his nose.

He popped the ice cream

into his mouth

and swallowed it.

Gulp.

"Gosh," said Mort,

"that was great.

I think vanilla ice cream

covered with ants

is my favorite flavor, too."

And Mort hurried off

to the snack cart

for more.